A Head Full of Stories

ReadZone Books Limited

First published in this edition 2015

© in this edition ReadZone Books Limited 2015
© in text Su Swallow 2005
© in illustrations Tim Archbold 2005

Su Swallow has asserted her right under the Copyright Designs and Patents Act 1988 to be identified as the author of this work.

Tim Archbold has asserted his right under the Copyright Designs and Patents Act 1988 to be identified as the illustrator of this work.

Every attempt has been made by the Publisher to secure appropriate permissions for material reproduced in this book. If there has been any oversight we will be happy to rectify the situation in future editions or reprints. Written submissions should be made to the Publisher.

British Library Cataloguing in Publication Data (CIP) is available for this title.

Printed in Malta by Melita Press.

ISBN 978 1 78322 456 2

Visit our website: www.readzonebooks.com

A Head Full of Stories

by Su Swallow
illustrated by Tim Archbold

READZONE

"Jack!"

"Story time!"

"No!" shouted Jack.
"My head is full up with stories."

"You tell me
a story, then."

So Jack told Mum about Cinderella.

He told Dad a story too.

And Grandma…

and Grandad…

and his brother…

and the cat...

and Teddy.

"My head's
empty now!"

26

"Tell me a story please!"

"Oh!"